STERLING CHILDREN'S BOOKS
New York

An Imprint of Sterling Publishing
387 Park Avenue South
New York, NY 10016

ISBN 978-1-4027-8338-8 (hardcover)

Library of Congress Cataloging-in-Publication Data Available
Distributed in Canada by Sterling Publishing
c/o Canadian Manda Group, 165 Dufferin Street
Toronto, Ontario, Canada M6K 3H6
Distributed in the United Kingdom by GMC Distribution Services
Castle Place, 166 High Street, Lewes, East Sussex, England BN7 1XU
Distributed in Australia by Capricorn Link (Australia) Pty. Ltd.
P.O. Box 704, Windsor, NSW 2756, Australia

For information about custom editions, special sales, and premium and corporate
purchases, please contact Sterling Special Sales at 800-805-5489
or specialsales@sterlingpublishing.com.

Printed in China
Lot #:
2 4 6 8 10 9 7 5 3 1
03/12

www.sterlingpublishing.com/kids

SILVER PENNY STORIES

Rapunzel

Told by Deanna McFadden
Illustrated by Ashley Mims

A man and his wife lived next to a wonderful garden guarded by a high wall. The garden belonged to a powerful old witch. Growing inside the garden was a beautiful patch of lettuce called rapunzel.

The wife thought it looked delicious and told her husband, "I'll die if I don't eat some rapunzel."

That night, her husband climbed over the wall and stole some of the witch's rapunzel for his wife. After she ate it, she wanted more. So, every night, her husband sneaked over to steal the witch's rapunzel.

One night, when the man climbed over the garden wall, the witch was waiting for him. "So you're the one stealing my rapunzel!" she shouted at him. Then she said, "In return for what you have stolen, you must promise to give me your firstborn child."

The man was too afraid to say no.

Soon after, the couple had a baby girl.

They named her Rapunzel.

Rapunzel's parents cried when the old witch came to take her, but the witch insisted that they keep their promise.

The witch took Rapunzel far away and locked her in a tower with neither a door nor stairs. There was only one tiny window at the top.

As time passed, Rapunzel's hair grew very long. Every day when the witch visited Rapunzel, she would call out, "Rapunzel, Rapunzel, let down your hair."

Then Rapunzel would let down her beautiful golden braid out the window, and the old witch would climb up. After her visit, the witch would climb back down the same way.

All alone in the tower, Rapunzel would sing. One day, a young prince heard her as he rode through the forest. He looked all around for a way into the tower but could not find one. Then he hid behind a tree and saw what happened when the witch shouted, "Rapunzel, Rapunzel, let down your hair."

Down came the braid. And up climbed the witch.

That's how you get into the tower, the prince thought.

After the witch left, he called, "Rapunzel, Rapunzel, let down your hair."

Down came the braid. And up climbed the prince.

"Who are you?" Rapunzel asked.

"I heard your beautiful singing and had to meet you," the prince said.

Rapunzel could tell that the prince was very kind. From that day on, he visited her every day after the witch left.

The prince fell deeply in love with Rapunzel, and she fell in love with him. One day, the prince asked Rapunzel to marry him. She said yes.

The next day the witch called out, "Rapunzel, Rapunzel, let down your hair."

Down came the braid. And up climbed the witch.

"Goodness," Rapunzel said. "You are much heavier than my prince."

"You wicked girl!" the old witch shouted. "I shut you away from the world so I would have you all to myself."

She grabbed Rapunzel's beautiful golden braid and cut it off with a pair of sharp scissors.

Then the witch closed her eyes and cast an awful spell that sent Rapunzel deep into the dark forest. Alone in the forest, Rapunzel cried and cried.

I will never see my prince again, she thought.

Meanwhile, the prince rode up to the tower on his horse.

He thought the witch was already gone, so he called out, "Rapunzel, Rapunzel, let down your hair."

The witch let the braid down for the prince to climb.

When the prince climbed through the window, he found the old witch waiting for him.

She said, "I've punished Rapunzel by sending her deep into the forest where you will never find her."

Then the powerful witch raised her
hands to cast an evil spell to punish
the prince. The prince jumped
out the window just in time, but
he landed on a prickly bush that
scratched his eyes.

The prince could no longer see, but he was determined to find Rapunzel. He went into the forest, tripping over roots and bumping into trees. Then one day, he heard a sweet voice singing.

Rapunzel! he thought.

The prince found her beside a brook. Rapunzel was so happy, she cried, and two of her tears dropped into the prince's eyes. The tears healed his eyes, and he could see once again.

Rapunzel and the prince returned to his kingdom where they married and lived happily ever after.